A G S   C L A S S I C S

Great American
Short Stories II

❧❧❧

Jack
LONDON

Stories retold by Joanne Suter
Illustrated by James Balkovek

AGS®

AMERICAN ... SANTA C... ... NC.
Cir... ...96

AGS CLASSICS

Great American Short Stories I

Washington Irving, Nathaniel Hawthorne, Mark Twain, Bret Harte, Edgar Allan Poe, Kate Chopin, Willa Cather, Sarah Orne Jewett, Sherwood Anderson, Charles W. Chesnutt

Great American Short Stories II

Herman Melville, Stephen Crane, Ambrose Bierce, Jack London, Edith Wharton, Charlotte Perkins Gilman, Frank R. Stockton, Hamlin Garland, O. Henry, Richard Harding Davis

Great British and Irish Short Stories

Arthur Conan Doyle, Saki (H. H. Munro), Rudyard Kipling, Katherine Mansfield, Thomas Hardy, E. M. Forster, Robert Louis Stevenson, H. G. Wells, John Galsworthy, James Joyce

Great Short Stories from Around the World

Guy de Maupassant, Anton Chekhov, Leo Tolstoy, Selma Lagerlöf, Alphonse Daudet, Mori Ogwai, Leopoldo Alas, Rabindranath Tagore, Fyodor Dostoevsky, Honoré de Balzac

Cover and Text Designer: Diann Abbott

Printed in the United States of America
Library of Congress Catalog Number 94-075025
ISBN 0-7854-0588-7
Product Number 40024
A 0 9 8 7 6 5 4 3 2

CONTENTS

❦ AGS Classic Short Stories ❧

*"The universe is made of
stories, not atoms."*
—Muriel Rukeyser

"The story's about you."
—Horace

Everyone loves a good story. It is hard
to think of a friendlier introduction to
classic literature. For one thing, short
stories are *short*—quick to get into and
easy to finish. Of all the literary forms,
the short story is the least intimidating
and the most approachable.

Great literature is an important part of
our human heritage. In the belief that
this heritage belongs to everyone, *AGS
Classic Short Stories* are adapted for
today's readers. Lengthy sentences and
paragraphs are shortened. Archaic words
are replaced. Modern punctuation and
spellings are used. Many of the longer
stores are abridged. In all the stories,

painstaking care had been taken to preserve the author's unique voice.

AGS Classic Short Stories have something for everyone. The hundreds of stories in the collection cover a broad terrain of themes, story types, and styles. Literary merit was a deciding factor in story selection. But no story was included unless it was as enjoyable as it was instructive. And special priority was given to stories that shine light on the human condition.

Each book in the *AGS Classic Short Stories* is devoted to the work of a single author. Little-known stories of merit are included with famous old favorites. Taken as a whole, the collected authors and stories make up a rich and diverse sample of the story-teller's art.

AGS Classic Short Stories guarantee a great reading experience. Readers who look for common interests, concerns, and experiences are sure to find them. Readers who bring their own gifts of perception and appreciation to the stories will be doubly rewarded.

❦ Jack London ❦
(1876–1916)

About the Author

Jack London held a number of interesting jobs in his short life. While still a teen-ager he was an oyster pirate in San Francisco Bay. At night he would go out on the bay and steal from other people's oyster beds. This illegal job almost got him killed. He also spent time as a janitor, a cannery worker, a hobo, a gold prospector, and a seaman. All of these experiences gave him material for his later writing.

Born in San Francisco, he was raised by his mother and stepsister Eliza. He grew up in Oakland, where his mother worked as a fortune-teller. He didn't care much for school. Most of his time was spent roaming the waterfront and reading. Even as a young boy he read constantly—up to 19 hours a day.

Before he was 20, he joined the gold rush to Alaska. His stepsister loaned him $1,500 for his trip to the Klondike. The only "gold" he found there were his wonderful adventures. These he turned into the stories that later made him famous. He is best known for his two novels *The Call of the Wild* (1903) and *White Fang* (1906). These stories show the struggle of man and beast against the powerful forces of nature.

Jack London lived as he wrote. He described his life as "raw and naked, wild and free." When he died, one of his friends said this of him: "Like Peter Pan, he never grew up. He could never hear of any kind of activity without wishing to take his share in it."

Jack London's works have been translated into more than 80 languages. His books are still popular all over the world. If you like action, adventure, and colorful settings, Jack London is for you.

A Daughter of the Aurora

Is a good woman hard to find? That was certainly so in the Alaskan frontier of 100 years ago. In this amusing story, a beautiful Frenchwoman has her choice between two men. Which one will win her hand? Will an exciting dogsled race settle the matter?

HERE THE WATER HAD FROZEN OVER. THE SURFACE WAS
AS FLAT, HARD, AND SLIPPERY AS A DANCE FLOOR.

A Daughter
of the Aurora

"Now you—how do you say it—lazy man! You lazy man want to have me for a wife. It is no good. Never, no never, will a lazy man be my husband!"

Thus Joy Molineau spoke her mind to Jack Harrington. The beautiful French woman said the same words she had said the night before to Louis Savoy.

"Listen, Joy...."

"No, no! Why must I listen to a lazy man? It is very bad. You hang around. You visit my cabin. You do nothing! How

11

would you ever feed a family? Why don't you have bags of gold dust? Other men have plenty!"

"But I work hard, Joy. Not a day goes by that I am not on the trail or up the creek. Even now I have just come off the trail. My dogs are still tired. Other men have luck. They find plenty of gold. I—I just don't have any luck."

"Ah! But when that fellow McCormack discovered gold on the Klondike, you did not go. Other men went. Other men are rich now!"

"You know I was hunting for gold over on the Tanana River," Harrington said. "I knew nothing of the Eldorado or Bonanza strikes until it was too late."

"That is different. Only you are—how do you say it—way off."

"What?"

"Way off. In the—yes—in the dark. It is never too late. One very rich mine is there, on the creek called Eldorado. A man staked his claim. He drove the stake and then he went away. No one knows what became of him. That man has just 60 days to file the papers on the claim. Then other men, plenty of other men—what do you call it—jump that claim. After 60 days they are going to race like the wind to file the papers. Whoever gets that claim will be very rich. That man will be able to feed his family!"

Harrington hid his excitement.

"When is the time up?" he asked. "Where exactly is the claim?"

"I talked to Louis Savoy last night," she continued, ignoring him. "He will, I think, be the winner."

"The heck with Louis Savoy!"

"Louis Savoy said in my cabin last night, 'Joy,' he said, 'I am a strong man. I have good dogs. I will be the winner. Then will you have me for a husband?' And I say to him—"

"What did you say?"

"I say, 'If Louis Savoy is the winner, then I will be his wife!'"

"And if he doesn't win?"

"Then Louis Savoy will not be—what do you call it—the father of my children."

"And if I win?"

"You the winner? Ha, ha! Never!"

Maddening as it was, Joy Molineau's laugh was pretty to hear. Harrington did not mind it. He had grown used to her ways. Besides, he was not the only one she treated this way. She teased all of her boyfriends. And very exciting she was, just then. Her lips were parted. Her face was rosy from the frosty cold. Her eyes were dancing with life. Her sled dogs gathered about her in a hairy mass. Their leader, Wolf Fang, laid his long snout softly in her lap.

"If I *do* win?" Harrington asked.

She looked from her dog to the man and back again.

"What do you say, Wolf Fang? If he is a strong man and files the papers, shall we become his wife? Eh? What do you say?"

Wolf Fang pricked up his ears. The big dog growled at Harrington.

"It is very cold," Joy suddenly cried. She rose to her feet and began to straighten out her dog team.

Harrington looked on calmly. She had kept him guessing from the first time they met. She had taught him to wait for what he wanted.

"Ai! Wolf Fang!" she cried. She sprang upon the sled as it leapt into sudden motion. "Ai! Ya! Mush on!"

From the corner of his eye, Harrington watched her swinging down the trail to Forty Mile. Where the road forked and crossed the river to Fort Cudahy, she halted the dogs. She turned about.

"Oh, Mister Lazy Man!" she called back. "Wolf Fang says yes—if you are the winner!"

Somehow, as such things will, the word leaked out. All of Forty Mile had been wondering about Joy Molineau's choice between her two boyfriends. Now folks made bets as to which man would win in the coming race. The camp divided itself into two groups. One group was helping Harrington. The other put every effort into seeing that Louis Savoy finished first.

There was a scramble for the best dogs. Good dogs were the most important key to a win. And a win meant plenty! It meant a woman as fine as any that had ever been created. It also meant a gold mine worth a million at least.

The news of McCormack's discovery on Bonanza had come down that fall. All the men in Lower Country, Circle City, and Forty Mile had rushed up the Yukon River. But Jack Harrington and Louis Savoy had been away looking for gold in the west.

Gold hunters staked moose pastures and creeks. Olaf Nelson laid claim to an unlikely creek called Eldorado. He posted his notice on 500 feet of the little creek. Then he disappeared. At the time, the nearest recording office was in the police barracks at Fort Cudahy. That was just across the river from Forty Mile. Eldorado Creek turned out to be a treasure house, but Olaf Nelson never made the trip to Fort Cudahy. He never filed his claim on the property.

Many men cast hungry eyes upon the claim. They knew the treasure was there, but they dared not touch it. The law said that 60 days could pass between the time when a claim was staked and when the papers were filed. During that time, no one else could touch the claim. The whole country knew that Olaf Nelson had disappeared. Scores of men were prepared to jump the claim at the end of the 60 days. Then they would race to Fort Cudahy to see who would be the first to file his papers.

At Forty Mile, however, only two men were in the contest for the Eldorado treasure. Everyone in the camp was

helping either Jack Harrington or Louis
Savoy. And each man needed help. It
was a stretch of more than 100 miles to
the recorder's office. The plan was that
Jack and Louis should each have four
relay teams of dogs. They would set off
with one team and have three more
stationed along the trail. Naturally, the
last relay team was the most important
one. Each man worked to find the
strongest possible sled dogs for that
final team. They bid on the finest
animals. Good dogs brought higher
prices than ever before.

The contest turned everyone's eyes
upon Joy Molineau—and not just
because she was the cause of it all. She
also owned the best sled dog in the
country. As wheel dog or leader, Wolf
Fang had no equal. The man whose sled
he led down that last stretch to Fort
Cudahy was bound to win. There could
be no doubt of it. The men of Forty Mile
sensed that it would be unfair for either

man to have such an advantage. So no one asked Joy to lend her dog.

The ways of women can be difficult to figure, however. The men of Forty Mile had no idea what tricks Joy Molineau was up to. Joy was a clever woman whose father had traded furs in that country before the gold-diggers ever arrived. She was a woman born beneath the *aurora borealis*—the sparkling northern lights. Afterwards, folks said that they had failed to appreciate Joy Molineau, this dark-eyed daughter of the aurora. She had a woman's understanding of men. They knew she played with them, but they did not know the wisdom of her play, its deepness and its skill. They saw only what Joy wanted them to see. Forty Mile never knew what was happening until Joy made her very last move.

Early in the week, the whole camp turned out to start Jack Harrington and Louis Savoy on their way. Both men planned to arrive at Eldorado Creek some days before the time ran out on Olaf Nelson's claim. That way, they could rest themselves and their dogs. Then they would be fresh for the first leg of the race toward the recording office in Fort Cudahy.

A couple of days after Harrington and Savoy left camp, Forty Mile began sending up the relay dog teams. One team would be stationed 75 miles from Fort Cudahy. The next one would be waiting at 50 miles, and the last just 25 miles from the finish.

Both teams for the last stretch of the run were powerful. As they prepared to leave camp, they seemed very equally matched. But at the last moment, Joy Molineau dashed in among them on her sled. She drew the man in charge of Harrington's team to one side. Hardly had the first words left her lips, when the man's mouth opened wide with surprise. He unhitched Wolf Fang from her sled and put the great dog at the head of Harrington's team. Then he mushed the string of animals into the Yukon trail.

"Poor Louis Savoy!" men said. But Joy Molineau said nothing. She flashed her black eyes and drove back to her father's cabin.

Midnight drew near. Olaf Nelson's claim was quickly running out. The temperature was 60 below zero. Scores of men had left their warm cabins in the hope of jumping Nelson's claim. Dressed from head to toe in fur, they had their notices ready for posting. Their dogs were standing ready for the run to the recording office. A patrol of mounted police had been put on duty to stop any trouble. The order was understood clearly by everyone. No man should place a stake until the last second of the day had ticked away.

The night was clear and cold. The aurora borealis painted colors across the sky. Rosy waves of light swept brightly across the heavens. Great sparkling bars of greenish white blotted out the stars. It was as if a giant's hand had drawn sweeping rainbows above the North Pole. And at this mighty show, the wolf dogs howled as wolves had howled since time began.

A fur-coated police officer stepped forward. He had a watch in his hand. The men worked among their dogs. They brought them to their feet, untangled their lines, straightened them out. The men firmly gripped their stakes and notices. Each and every man had gone over the boundaries of the claim so often that he could now have done it with his eyes closed. The police officer raised his hand. The men came to attention.

"Time! Go!"

The crowd of men shot forward. Round the claim they ran. They stuck notices at every corner and down the middle where the two center stakes were to be planted. Then they sprang for the sleds on the frozen bed of the creek. The air was filled with sound and motion. Sled ran into sled. With bristling manes and bared fangs, the dog teams tangled with each other. The narrow creek became a struggling mass of sleds. Dog whips sang out. One by one the sleds crept out and shot from sight in the darkness.

Jack Harrington had expected this crush. He waited by his sled until it was over. Louis Savoy respected Harrington's know-how as a dog driver. He was following his rival's lead—so he also waited. The rest of the racers were far ahead when Harrington and Savoy took to the trail. They sped ten miles or so down to Bonanza Creek before they came upon the others. The men who had gone before were now close together, racing along in single file.

There was little or no chance of one sled passing another at that stage. The sleds measured 16 inches wide. The trail was only 18 inches wide and packed down at least a foot. It was like a gutter. On each side spread a blanket of soft snow. If a man turned into the soft snow while trying to pass, his dogs would be in it up to their bellies. They would be slowed to a snail's pace. So the men waited. There were no changes in position over the 15 miles to Dawson. There the relay teams were waiting.

Both Harrington and Savoy were willing to drive their first teams to death if necessary. They had their fresh teams placed a couple of miles beyond those of the other racers. While the others changed sleds and teams, they kept going, shooting on to the broad Yukon.

Soon they came to a dangerous stretch of the river. Here the water had frozen over to a surface that was as flat, hard, and slippery as a dance floor. The second his sled struck this ice, Harrington came to his knees. He held on with one hand.

His whip sang fiercely among his dogs and he shouted at them.

Then Savoy's team seemed to be catching up. The two teams spread out on the smooth surface. Each strained to keep the pace. But few men of the North could move their dogs as well as Jack Harrington could. At once he began to pull ahead. Louis Savoy desperately tried to keep pace. But his lead dogs were running even with the tail of Harrington's sled.

Midway on the glassy stretch, their relay teams shot out from the bank. But Harrington did not slow his pace. He watched for his chance when the new sled swung in close. Then he leaped across, shouting as he did so to quicken the pace of his fresh dogs. The relay driver fell off and skidded away.

Savoy made the same moves with his teams. The tired dogs were without drivers now. They went right and left, running into each other and piling up on the ice. Harrington kept in the lead with his fresh team. Savoy hung on right behind him. As they neared the end of the smooth ice, both of them shot onto the narrow trail between the soft snowbanks. They led the race. The folks of Dawson, watching by the light of the aurora, swore that they had never seen such driving.

At 60 below zero, men cannot live long without fire or hard exercise. So Harrington and Savoy began a way of driving known as "ride and run." After every mile or so, they jumped from their sleds. With lines still in hand, they ran behind until their blood pumped fast enough to drive away the cold. Then they jumped back to the sleds and rode until their body heat ran out again. In this way, riding and running, they covered the second and third relays.

Several times, on smooth ice, Savoy tried to pass. He failed each time. Strung along for five miles behind them, the remainder of the racers tried to catch up. But they could not. Only Louis Savoy was keeping up with Jack Harrington's killing pace.

As they swung into the last station, Harrington's final relay team dashed alongside him. When he saw Wolf Fang in the lead, he knew that the race was his. No team in the North could pass him on those last 25 miles. And when Savoy saw Wolf Fang heading Harrington's team, he knew that he was out of the running. He swore softly to himself, but he still clung to Harrington's trail. While there was still a chance, he would not give up. The two teams raced along as the day broke in the southeast. And the two men wondered in joy and sorrow at that which Joy Molineau had done.

The people of Forty Mile woke early to gather near the edge of the trail. From this point they could see the up-Yukon course. Here they could also see across the river to the finish. There, at Fort Cudahy, the gold recorder waited. Joy Molineau also waited, a bit back from the trail where fires had been built. Men had begun making their bets. They bet gold dust and sled dogs, and the odds were on Wolf Fang.

"Here they come!" shouted a boy who had climbed to the top of a pine tree.

Up the Yukon, a black dot appeared against the snow. It was followed closely by a second. As these first two dots grew larger, more of the black dots showed themselves—but these were far to the rear. Soon the dots could be seen as dogs and sleds, and men lying flat upon them.

"Wolf Fang leads," a police officer whispered to Joy. She smiled back at him, her eyes flashing.

"Ten to one on Harrington!" a gambler cried out. He took out his sack of gold dust and held it up.

Joy looked at the officer. "You don't make much money, do you?" she asked.

The police officer shook his head.

"You have some dust? Ah, how much?" asked Joy.

The police officer showed Joy his own sack of gold dust. She measured it quickly with her eyes.

"Maybe 200, eh? Good. Now I'll give you a—what do you call it—a tip. Cover the bet." Joy smiled a secret smile. The police officer thought about it. He looked up the trail. The two men had risen to their knees. They were lashing their dogs furiously. Harrington was in the lead.

"Ten to one on Harrington!" shouted the gambler. He waved his sack in the police officer's face.

"Cover the bet," Joy repeated.

The police officer obeyed. He shook his head to show that he gave in not to his own reason, but to Joy's charm. Joy nodded. She smiled to make him feel that he had done the right thing.

All noise stopped. Men quit placing their bets.

The sleds swept wildly upon them. Though his lead dog was right on the tail of Harrington's sled, Louis Savoy's face was without hope. Harrington's mouth was set. He looked neither to the right nor to the left. His dogs were leaping in perfect rhythm. They were firm-footed. Wolf Fang, head low, was leading his team beautifully.

The people of Forty Mile stood breathless. The only sounds were the roar of the sled runners and the song of the whips.

Then the clear voice of Joy Molineau rose in the air. "Ai! Ya! Wolf Fang! Wolf Fang!"

Wolf Fang heard. He left the trail sharply, heading directly for his mistress. The team dashed after him. The sled tipped onto a single runner, shooting

Harrington into the snow. Savoy went by like a flash. Harrington slowly got to his feet and watched his rival skimming across the river to the gold recorder's. He could not help hearing what was said.

"Ah, Harrington did very well," Joy Molineau was explaining to the police officer. "He—what do you call it—set the pace. Yes, he set the pace very well."

A Piece of
Steak

This is a portrait of a
prize fighter who is past
his prime. Every opponent
he meets is younger and
stronger. What do you
suppose he thinks and feels
about his life? Read on to
find out.

HE KNEW THE BLOWS FOR WHAT THEY WERE—TOO
QUICK TO BE DANGEROUS. SANDEL WANTED TO RUSH
THINGS. IT WAS THE WILD WAY OF YOUTH.

A Piece of Steak

With his last bit of bread, Tom King mopped up the last of the flour gravy. He wiped his plate clean and chewed the final bite slowly. When he arose from the table, he was struck by the feeling that he was still very hungry.

Yet he alone had eaten. The two children in the other room had been sent early to bed. His wife hoped that, in sleep, they might forget that they had gone without supper. She herself had touched nothing. She had sat silently and watched him with worried eyes. She was a thin, worn woman of the working class. Yet even now it was clear she had once been very pretty. The flour for the gravy she had borrowed from the neighbor across the hall. The last two pennies had gone to buy the bread.

The big man sat down by the window on a shaky chair that groaned under his weight. There was nothing more to eat, so he folded his empty hands in his lap. His movements were heavy, as though they were slowed by the weight of his muscles. He was a solid, sturdy-looking man. His rough clothes were old and baggy. The uppers of his shoes were thin and there were holes in the bottoms. He wore a cheap cotton shirt with a worn collar and dark paint stains.

But it was Tom King's face that showed clearly what he was. It was the face of a prize fighter. It was the face of one who had spent long years in the ring. It was a dark, dangerous face. King had lips that cut like a gash in his face. The jaw was heavy and fierce. The eyes moved slowly under heavy lids and shaggy brows. He was like an animal, and the eyes were the most animal-like feature about him. They were like the eyes of a sleepy lion, the eyes of a fighting beast. The close-cut hair showed every bump on his head. His nose had been broken twice and its shape changed by many blows. One ear was always swollen to twice its size. Though he had just shaved, a beard already showed blue-black on his skin.

Altogether, it was the face of a man to be afraid of in a dark alley or lonely place. And yet Tom King was not a bad man. He had never done anything against the law. He had never been known to pick a fight and had harmed no one. He was a professional. His strength and power were only for use in the ring. Outside the ring he was slow-going, easy-natured.

In his younger days, he had ready money. But he shared it with friends too often for his own good. He disliked no one and had few enemies. Fighting was a business with him. In the ring he struck to hurt. He struck to destroy. But there was no anger in it. It was a plain business deal. People gathered and paid to see men knock each other out. The winner took home the money.

When Tom King faced the Gouger, 20 years before, he knew that the Gouger's jaw had been broken in his last fight. The break had only just healed. Yet he had swung at that jaw over and over. He broke it again in the ninth round.

King did not break it because of any ill will toward the Gouger, but because that was the surest way to end the fight and win the money. Nor had the Gouger borne him any ill will for doing it. It was the game. Both knew the game and were willing to play it.

Tom King had never been a talker. Now he sat by the window, silent, staring at his hands. The veins stood out large and swollen on the backs of the hands. The knuckles were smashed and battered. They showed the use to which they had been put. Tom King knew the meaning of those big veins. His heart had pumped too much blood through them at top pressure. Those hands could no longer do their work well. And he tired easily now. No longer could he do a fast 20 rounds—fight, fight, fight from gong to gong. No longer could he be beaten to the ropes and then come back strong in that last, 20th round. No longer could he bring the yelling crowd to their feet as he rained down showers of blows. No longer could his heart keep pumping the blood through perfect veins. He stared at his hands now, at the battered knuckles and the big veins. For just a moment he saw them as they once were—young and fine. He saw his hands as they had looked before the first knuckle had been smashed. That had been on the head of Benny Jones, otherwise known as the Welsh Terror.

A feeling of hunger came back to him.

"Oh, but couldn't I go for a piece of steak!" he muttered aloud. He clenched his huge fists and swore out loud.

"I tried the butcher shops," said his wife quietly.

"And they wouldn't?" he asked.

"Not a cent. The butcher said—" She stopped in the middle of her sentence.

"Go on. What did he say?"

"He said he was thinking Sandel would beat you tonight. He said you already owed him money as it was."

Tom King grunted. He did not reply. He was thinking about the bull terrier dog he had owned in his younger days. He'd fed that dog steaks without end. The butcher would have given him credit for a thousand steaks—*then*. But times had changed. Tom King was getting old. And old men, fighting second-rate fights, couldn't expect to run bills of any size with the shops.

He had gotten up that morning with a longing for a piece of steak. That longing had not gone away. He had not had proper training for this fight. It was a dry year in Australia. Times were tough and jobs were hard to find. He had had no practice fights. His food had not been of the best, and there had not been enough of it. He had done a few days of work at the ship yards when he could get it, and had run in the early mornings to get his legs in shape. But it was hard training alone. It was hard training when you had a wife and two kids that must be fed.

Now and then he had borrowed some money from old pals. But the dry year made things tough for them, too. The fight club had advanced him the loser's end of the fight money. Yet even so, he was not ready. His training had not been good enough. He should have had better food and no worries. Besides, when a man is 40, it is harder to get into shape than when he is 20.

"What time is it, Lizzie?" he asked.

His wife went across the hall to ask. Then she came back.

"Quarter before eight."

"They'll be starting the first fight in a few minutes," he said. "Then there's two more before mine. I don't come on for over an hour."

Another silent ten minutes passed. Then he rose to his feet.

"Truth is, Lizzie, I ain't had proper training."

He reached for his hat and started for the door. He did not turn to kiss her. He never did before going out. But on this night she threw her arms around him. She pulled him down close to her face. She seemed quite small against the huge man.

"Good luck, Tom," she said. "You've got to beat him."

"Yep, I've got to beat him," he repeated. "That's all there is to it. I've just got to beat him."

He laughed with pretended cheer. She pressed more closely against him. Across her shoulders he looked around the bare room. It was all he had in the world—just this room with the rent due, and her and the kids. And he was leaving it to go out into the night to get meat for his mate and cubs. He was not like a modern working man going to run a machine. In the old, wild, royal, animal way, he was fighting for his living.

"I've got to beat him," he repeated. There was quiet hope in his voice. "If it's a win, it's enough money to pay all we owe with a lump of money left over.

If it's a loss, I get nothing, not even a penny for me to ride home on the train. I've already gotten all that's coming to the loser. Good-by, old woman. I'll come straight home if I win."

"I'll be waiting up," she called to him along the hall.

It was a full two miles to the boxing ring. As he walked along he remembered when he had been the heavyweight champ of New South Wales. In those days he would have ridden in a cab to the fight. Most likely, some fan would have paid for the cab and ridden along with him. Now he walked! And, as any man knew, a hard two miles was not the best way to prepare for a fight.

He was an old one, and the world did not smile on old ones. He was good for nothing now except shipyard work. His broken nose and swollen ear made it hard to get even those jobs. He found himself wishing that he had learned a trade. It would have been better in the long run. But no one had told him. And he knew, deep down in his heart, that he would not have listened if they had.

It had been so easy. There had been big money, sharp fights, plenty of time for rest and fun in between. There had been eager fans, slaps on the back, shakes of the hand. Fellows were glad to buy him a meal for just five minutes of talk. Best of all, there had been the glory of it—the yelling crowds, the referee's "the Winner!" and his name on the sports page the next day.

Those had been times! But it came to him now, in his slow, thoughtful way, that it was the old ones he had been beating then. He was Youth, rising. They were Age, sinking. No wonder it had been easy. They were the ones with swollen veins and battered hands. They were tired in the bones from the long battles they had already fought.

He remembered the time he had put down old Stowsher Bill in the 18th round. Old Bill had cried like a baby afterward in the dressing room. Perhaps old Bill's rent had been due. Perhaps he'd had a wife and a couple of kids. And perhaps Bill, that very day of the fight, had been hungry for a piece of steak. Bill had fought the game. He had taken the blows. Young Tom King had fought for glory and easy money that night 20 years ago. He could see now, after he had gone through it all himself, that Bill had fought for a bigger stake. No wonder old Bill had cried afterward in the dressing room.

Well, a man had only so many fights in him. It was the iron law of the game. One man might have 100 hard fights in him. Another man might have only 20. Each had a set number—and when he had fought them he was done. Yes, he had had more fights in him than most of them. He had had far more than his share of the hard fights, the kind that worked the heart and lungs to bursting.

He'd had plenty of the kind that wore out nerve and strength and made brain and bones tired. Yes, he had done better than all of them. None of his old fighting partners were left now. He was the last of the old ones. He had seen them all finished. And he had had a hand in finishing some of them.

The boxing clubs had tried him out against the old ones. One after another, he had put them away. He'd laughed when—like old Bill—they cried in the dressing room. And now he was an old one himself. Now they tried out the youngsters on him.

There was this fellow Sandel. He had come over from New Zealand with a record of wins behind him. But nobody in Australia knew much about him. So they put him up against old Tom King. If Sandel won, he would be given better men to fight and more money to win. He would put up a fierce battle. He had everything to win—money and glory and a name. It was all ahead of him. Tom King was the old fellow who guarded the highway to fame and fortune. And Tom had nothing to win but enough to pay the landlord and the shop keepers.

Tom pictured the form of youth. It was firm of muscle and smooth of skin. He saw youth with heart and lungs that had never been tired and torn. Yes, youth was the enemy. It destroyed the old ones. Youth did not see that in doing so, it slowly destroyed itself, wearing out its heart and smashing its hands.

Tom turned left. He walked three more blocks and came to the boxing arena. A crowd of young fellows hanging outside the door made way for him. He heard one say to another, "That's him! That's Tom King!"

Inside, on the way to his dressing room, a young fan shook his hand.

"How are you feeling, Tom?" he asked.

"Fit as a fiddle," King answered. But he knew he lied. He knew that if he had any money he would give it right there for a good piece of steak.

He came out of the dressing room and walked down to the square ring in the center of the hall. A cheer went up from the waiting crowd. He nodded right and left, though he knew few of the faces. Most were the faces of kids not even born when he was winning his first fights in the ring. He leaped lightly to the raised platform. Ducking through the ropes to his corner, he sat down on a folding stool.

Jack Ball, the referee, came over. He shook his hand. Ball was a broken-down boxer who had not entered the ring as a fighter for ten years. King was glad that he had him for referee. They were both old ones. If he should break a few rules with Sandel, he knew Ball would let it pass.

The audience cheered and cheered again as Sandel himself sprang through the ropes. The young fighter sat down in his corner. Tom King looked across the

ring at him. In a few minutes they would
be locked together in a fight. Each would
try with all the force he had for a knockout. Right now King could see little of
the man. Sandel, like himself, wore long
pants and a big sweater over his ring
costume. His face was powerful and
handsome. His wide neck hinted at the
strength of the rest of his body.

Tom King was unable to shake the
vision of youth from his eyes. Always now
there were youngsters rising up in the
boxing game. And always there were old
ones going down before them. The young
ones climbed to the top over the bodies
of the old ones. Ever they came, more and
more youngsters. And ever they put the
old ones away. Then they, themselves,
became old ones and traveled the same
downward path. And ever behind them,
pressing on them, was youth—the new
babies, dragging the old ones down. And
behind them, more babies to the end of

time. Youth must always have its way and will never die.

King looked over to the press box and he nodded to the newsmen. Then he held out his hands. His helpers slipped on his gloves and laced them tight. In the other corner, Sandel's pants and sweater were pulled off. Tom King looked over. He saw pure youth with heavy muscles that slipped and slid like live things under the white satin skin. Sandel's whole young body was crawling with life. Tom King knew that it was a life that had not yet poured out its strength during long fights.

The two men left their corners to meet each other. As the gong sounded, they shook hands. Then they quickly took their fighting positions. Suddenly, like a machine of steel and springs, Sandel was in and out and in again. He landed a left to the eye, a right to the ribs. He ducked a swing. Then he danced lightly away and close back in again. He was fast and clever.

It was a great show. The house yelled and cheered. But King was not dazzled. He had fought too many fights and too many youngsters. He knew the blows for what they were—too quick to be very dangerous. Sandel was going to rush things right from the start. It was the wild way of youth.

Sandel darted in and out, here, there, and everywhere. He was light-footed and eager-hearted. Without effort, he leaped from move to move. And every move was centered upon destroying Tom King. Tom King stood between him and fortune.

Tom King waited, for he knew his business. He understood youth. There was nothing to do until the other lost some of his steam, he thought. He grinned to himself as he ducked so a heavy blow would land on the top of his head. King could have ducked lower. If he had, the blow would have harmlessly whizzed past. But he remembered his own early fights and how he smashed his first knuckle on the head of the Welsh Terror. He was playing that game. That duck got one of Sandel's knuckles. Not that Sandel would mind it now. He would go on hitting as hard as ever through this fight. But later he would miss that knuckle. Then he would look back and remember how he had smashed it on Tom King's head.

The first round was all Sandel's. He had the crowd cheering for his fast rushes. He rained punches on King, and King did nothing. He never struck once. He only covered up, blocked and ducked. Sometimes he shook his head when a punch landed. But he never leaped about or wasted an ounce of strength. All King's moves were well-planned. His heavy, slow-moving eyes made him appear to be half asleep or dazed. Yet they were eyes that saw everything. They had been trained to see everything through more than 20 years in the ring. Tom King's eyes did not blink before a coming blow. They coolly saw and measured distance.

Then it was the end of the round. He was back in his corner for a minute's rest. He lay back. His legs stretched long and his arms rested on the ropes. His chest and stomach rose and fell. He gulped down the air fanned by towels. He listened with closed eyes to the voices of the crowd. "Why don't you fight, Tom?" many were crying. "Afraid of him, are you?"

"Muscle bound!" he heard one man say. "He can't move any quicker. Put my money on Sandel."

The gong struck. The two men left their corners. Sandel came forward past the center of the ring. He was eager to begin again. But King was happy to move in the shorter distance. He was saving energy. He had not trained well. He had not had enough to eat. Every step counted. Besides, he had already walked two miles to ringside.

The second round was just like the first. Sandel attacked like a whirlwind. The crowd yelled loudly, demanding to know why King would not fight. Beyond ducking and delivering some slow blows, he did nothing but block and stall and clinch. Sandel wanted a faster pace. But King was wise. He refused to speed up. There was a sad grin on his ring-battered face. And he went on saving his strength. Sandel threw *his* strength away. King was in charge. He watched with cool eyes and head. He moved slowly, waiting for Sandel to tire. To most of the crowd, it looked as though King was hopelessly beaten. They called out their bets on Sandel. But there were a few wise ones who knew King from the old days. They kept their money on King.

The third round began as usual, one-sided. Sandel was doing all the punching. A half minute had passed when the young man carelessly left an opening. King's eyes and right arm flashed in the same instant. It was his first real blow, a hook, with all the weight of his body behind it. It was like a sleepy lion suddenly flashing out a paw. Sandel was caught on the side of the jaw. He fell like an injured bull. The crowd gasped. The old man was not muscle-bound after all! He could drive a blow like a hammer.

Sandel was shaken. He rolled over. He tried to get up. But the sharp yell from his corner told him to take the count. He knelt on one knee, ready to rise. He waited while the referee stood over him, counting the seconds loudly in his ear. At the count of nine, he rose. He stood ready to fight.

Tom King, facing him, was sorry that the blow had not been an inch nearer the point of the jaw. That would have been a knockout. He could have carried home the winnings to the wife and kids.

The round continued to the end of its three minutes. King was as slow and sleepy-eyed as ever. But Sandel, for the first time, showed him respect. As the round neared its close, King worked the fight around to his own corner. Then, when the gong struck, he sat down quickly on the waiting stool. Sandel had to walk all the way across the ring to his own corner.

It was just a little thing. But, put all together, it was the little things that counted. Sandel was forced to walk that many more steps, to give up that much more energy. He lost a part of that all-important minute of rest. At the beginning of every round King moved slowly out of his corner. That way he forced the other fighter to move the greater distance. The end of every round found King near his own corner so that he could sit right down.

Two more rounds went by. King saved his energy. Sandel wasted his. The young man landed a good number of blows and the crowd called for King to go in and fight. Yet King kept on in his dogged slowness.

Again, in the sixth round, Sandel was careless. Again Tom King's fearful right flashed out to the jaw. And again Sandel took the nine-count.

By the seventh round Sandel was no longer at full strength. He settled down to what he knew was to be the hardest fight of his life. Tom King was an old one—but a better old one than he had ever met. He was an old one who never lost his head, whose blows fell like a club, and who had a knockout in either hand. Nevertheless, Tom King dared not hit often. He never forgot his battered knuckles. Every hit must count if the knuckles were to last out the fight.

Just before the eighth round, King sat in his corner looking over at Sandel. The thought came to him that his wisdom and Sandel's youth put together would make a world's champion heavyweight. But Sandel would never become a world champion. He did not have the wisdom. And the only way for him to get it was to buy it with youth. Once wisdom was his, youth would be gone. One would have to be spent to buy the other.

King used everything he knew. He often held Sandel in a clinch, his shoulder driving stiffly into the other fighter's ribs. King knew that a shoulder blow was as good as a punch. It could do just as much harm, and it used up a lot less energy. Also in the clinches, King rested his weight on Sandel and would not let go. This always brought in the referee, who tore them apart. Sandel used his force to pull away. He had not yet learned to rest. He could not stop himself from using those strong muscles and flying arms. In every clinch Sandel would swing his right behind his own back and into King's face. The crowd loved the move, but it was not dangerous. It was, in fact, just that much wasted strength. But Sandel was tireless. He did not know the limits of his energy. King grinned and stood the pain.

Sandel began pounding some fierce rights to the body. It appeared that King was taking some terrible blows. Only the old-timers in the crowd saw the clever punch of King's left glove to Sandel's upper arm just before each blow. It was true that the blow landed each time. But each time it was robbed of its power by King's punch on the arm.

In the ninth round—three times in one minute—King's right fist hooked to Sandel's jaw. And three times Sandel's heavy body fell to the mat. Each time he took the nine-count and then rose to his feet. The young man was shaken but still strong. He had lost much of his speed, but he was wasting less effort. And he still had youth in his favor.

King had experience on his side. He replaced lost energy with wisdom born of many long fights. Through the years he had learned to make every move count. He had also learned how to draw the other fighter's punches, to get him to throw his strength away. King rested, but he never let Sandel rest. It was a trick of age and experience.

Early in the tenth round, King began stopping the other's rushes with straight left jabs to the face. Sandel was more careful now. He answered by drawing the left, then ducking it and delivering his right in a swinging hook to the side of the head. It was too high up to do any real harm. But when first the blow landed, King saw an old familiar black curtain begin to fall across his mind. For just a bit of an instant, he stopped. Sandel and the crowd of white, watching faces disappeared. Then, in the next moment he saw the crowd again. It was as if he had slept for a time and just opened his eyes. The instant of darkness was so short that there had been no time for him to fall. The crowd saw him totter. They saw his knees give. But then they saw him recover and tuck his chin deeper into the safety of his left shoulder.

Several times Sandel repeated the blow. The battering kept King a bit dazed. Then he began to attack in return. He cut upward with the whole strength of his right arm. The swing was timed perfectly. It landed squarely on Sandel's face just as he was ducking down. Sandel's whole body lifted in the air and curled backward. He struck the mat on his head and shoulders. Twice this worked for King. Then he turned loose and hammered Sandel to the ropes. He gave the man no chance to rest or to set himself. King smashed in blow upon blow until the crowd rose to its feet. The air was filled with the roar of the cheers.

But Sandel was strong. He stayed on his feet even though a knockout seemed certain. An official, worried by the dreadful blows, rose to his feet to stop the fight. But the gong struck for the end of the round, and Sandel dragged himself to his corner. He called to the official that he could continue.

Tom King leaned back in his corner. Disappointed, he was breathing hard. If the fight had been stopped, the referee probably would have given him the decision. The prize money would have been his. Unlike Sandel, he was not fighting for glory or career. He was fighting for the money. And now Sandel would have a minute of rest.

Youth will be served—this saying flashed into King's mind. He remembered the first time he had heard it. It was the night he had put away old Bill. The fan who had bought him a drink after the fight had used those words. *Youth will be served!* The fan was right. And on that night long ago he had *been* youth. Tonight youth sat in the other corner. As for himself, he had been fighting for half an hour now, and he was an old man. If he had fought like Sandel, he would not have lasted 15 minutes. But the point was—now he could not gather his strength back. His legs were heavy underneath him, and they were beginning to cramp. He should not have walked those two miles to the fight. And there was the steak which he had been longing for that morning. A great and terrible hatred rose up in him for the butcher who had refused him credit. It was hard for an old man to go into a fight without enough to eat. And a piece of steak was such a little thing. It cost a few pennies at most, yet it meant everything to him.

The gong sounded to open the 11th round. Sandel rushed forward. He made a show of energy which he did not really have. King knew it was a bluff. He clinched in close. Then, going free, he let Sandel get set. It was what King wanted.

He pretended to throw a left. Sandel ducked and swung upward with a hook. Then King took a half step backward. He delivered an uppercut full to the face. Sandel fell to the mat. After that, King never let him rest. He took blows himself, but dealt far more. He smashed Sandel to the ropes, hooking and driving into him. And when Sandel would have fallen, King caught him with one hand. With the other, he smashed him into the ropes where he could not fall.

The crowd by this time was going mad. Nearly every voice was yelling, "Go to it, Tom!" "Get him! Get him!" "You've got him, Tom!" It was to be a whirlwind finish, and that was what a ringside crowd paid to see.

And Tom King, who for half an hour had saved his strength, now used it. It was the one great effort he knew he had in him. It was his one chance—now or not at all. His strength was going fast. He hoped that before the last of it went

out of him, he could beat Sandel down
for the count. As he continued to strike,
he realized how hard a man Sandel was
to knock out. He had the strength of
youth in him. And he was tough as well
as young. Only out of such strength were
real fighters made.

Sandel was reeling and staggering.
But Tom King's legs were cramping. His
knuckles were going bad on him. Yet he
forced himself to strike more blows.
Every one brought the fire of pain to his
hands. Now he was taking fewer blows
himself—but he was weakening as
quickly as Sandel. His blows hit their
mark, but there was no longer weight
behind them. Each blow was a huge
effort. His legs were like lead. They
dragged under him. Sandel's fans saw
this, and they cheered for their man.

King gave a burst of pure effort. He
delivered two blows in a row. He threw a
left, a bit too high, to the stomach. It was
followed by a right cross to the jaw. They

were not heavy blows. But Sandel was weak and dazed. He went down and lay still. The referee stood over him. He shouted the count of seconds in his ear. If he did not rise before the tenth second was called, the fight was lost. The crowd stood in hushed silence. King rested on shaking legs. He was dizzy now. Before his eyes swirled the sea of faces. To his ears, as from a far away distance, came the count of the referee. Yet he looked upon the fight as his. It was impossible that a man so badly beaten could rise.

Only youth could rise, and Sandel rose. At the fourth second he rolled over on his face. He felt blindly for the ropes. By the seventh second he had dragged himself to one knee. There he rested, his head nodding and rolling on his shoulders. As the referee cried, "Nine!" Sandel stood up. His left arm was wrapped about his face. His right guarded his stomach. He came toward King, hoping for a clinch and more time.

At the instant Sandel rose, King was at him. But the two blows he delivered fell on Sandel's arms. The next moment Sandel was in the clinch, holding on tight. The referee tried to drag the two men apart. King helped to force himself free. He knew how quickly youth rested. He knew that Sandel was his if he could keep him from resting. One stiff punch would do it. *Sandel was his.* He had outfought him.

Sandel pulled out of the clinch. King knew that one good blow would knock him over and down and out. In a flash of anger, he remembered the piece of steak. He wished that he had it then behind the next punch he must deliver. He readied himself for the blow. But it was not heavy enough or fast enough. Sandel swayed but did not fall. He staggered back to the ropes and held on. King staggered after him and delivered another blow. But his own body had turned on him. All that was left was a mind dimmed and clouded by weariness. The blow was aimed for the jaw. It struck no higher than the shoulder. He had willed the blow higher, but his tired arms had not been able to obey. Tom King himself stepped back and nearly fell. Once again he tried. This time his punch missed altogether. From weakness he fell against Sandel. They clinched. King held on to save himself from sinking to the floor.

King did not try to free himself. He had used all that he had. He was gone. And youth had been served. Even in the clinch, he could feel Sandel growing stronger against him. When the referee pushed them apart—there, before his eyes, he saw youth at the ready again. From instant to instant Sandel grew stronger. His punches, weak at first, became stronger.

Tom King's blurred eyes saw the gloved fist driving at his jaw. He wanted to guard it with his arm. He saw the danger. He willed the arm to act. But the arm was too heavy. It seemed to be made of lead. It would not lift itself, though he tried to lift it with all his soul. Then the gloved fist landed home. King felt a sharp snap like an electric spark. A curtain of darkness fell around him.

When he opened his eyes again he was in his corner. He heard the yelling of the crowd like the roar of the sea. A wet cloth was being pressed against the back of his neck. Someone was blowing cold water in a spray over his face and chest. His gloves had already been removed. And Sandel was bending over him shaking his hand. He felt no anger toward the man who had knocked him out. He returned the handshake though it made his battered knuckles hurt.

Then Sandel stepped to the center of the ring. The crowd grew silent to hear him accept the next challenge. King looked on without much interest. His helpers dried his face and prepared him to leave the ring. He felt hungry. It was not the usual kind of hunger, but a great faintness. It was a deep pain at the pit of his stomach. He remembered back into the fight. He recalled the moment when he had Sandel at the point of defeat. Ah, that piece of steak would have done it! He had needed just one more good blow. But it wasn't there, and he had lost. It was all because of the piece of steak.

He tore free of any help as he ducked through the ropes. Jumping heavily to the floor, he pushed his way through the crowd. As he was leaving the dressing room for the street, a young fellow spoke to him.

"Why didn't you just go in and get him when you had him?" the young fellow asked.

"Aw, get out of my way!" said Tom King. He passed down the steps to the sidewalk.

The doors of the tavern at the corner were swinging wide. He saw the lights. He heard the many voices talking about the fight. He heard the clink of money on the bar. Somebody called to him to have a drink. He stopped, then refused and went on his way.

He did not have a cent in his pocket. The two-mile walk home seemed very long. He was certainly getting old. Near the bridge, he sat down suddenly on a bench. He thought of his wife sitting up for him. She would be waiting to learn the outcome of the fight. That was harder than any knockout. It seemed almost impossible to face.

He felt weak and sore. His smashed knuckles hurt. Even if he could find a job at the shipyards, it would be a week before he could hold a shovel. The hunger twisting in the pit of his stomach was sickening. A terrible wave of misery came over him. Into his eyes came unwanted tears. He covered his face with his hands—and as he cried, he remembered old Bill. He remembered how he had beaten him that night so long ago. Poor old Bill! He could understand now why Bill had cried in his dressing room.

Thinking About
the Stories

A Daughter of the Aurora

1. All stories fit into one or more categories. Is this story serious or funny? Would you call it an adventure, a love story, or a mystery? Is it a character study? Or is it simply a picture the author has painted of a certain time and place? Explain your thinking.

2. An author builds the plot around the conflict in a story. In this story, what forces or characters are struggling against each other? How is the conflict finally resolved?

3. Compare and contrast at least two characters in this story. In what ways are they alike? In what ways are they different?

A Piece of Steak

1. The plot is the series of events that takes place in a story. Usually, story events are linked in some way. Can you name an event in this story that was the cause of a later event?

2. What period of time is covered in this story—an hour, a week, several years? What role, if any, does time play in the story?

3. Suppose this story had a completely different outcome. Can you think of another effective ending for this story?